"Lewis' gripping tale, at under 100 pages, will keep readers guessing throughout. [It] deftly takes readers to another world…an inviting…tale of the desire to uncover a lost myth."

-*Kirkus Reviews*

"…an ancient, yet timeless, fairy tale of curiosity, discovery, and corruption. The narrators' perspective plays with your mind…It begs the question if this cycle of their goddess will repeat. The answer is as sharp as a panther's canines."

-Miriam Meeks, Manager, *Middleberg Books*

"*The Archivist* is a gem in a sea of stones. Alicia Cahalane Lewis captures the essence of the Divine Feminine and the origins in a way that portrays what and who SHE truly is. I felt HER essence come through in the most unassuming way; it was the vulnerability and humility that resonates through every cell."

-Sarah Michelle Wergin, RN,LAc, Teacher, Author of *Awaken-The Alchemy of Divine Union*

Have you ever wondered how legends get created?

Alicia Cahalane Lewis's gorgeous new novella, *The Archivist*, imagines how the first feline goddess, the black panther, found her way into the stories and legends of ancient Mesopotamia, Greece, and Egypt.

Narrated in first person plural by a band of roaming nomads who are the first to worship the goddess, they are compelled to honor their black panther, who has dropped into their lives unexpectedly, by building the first feline sphinx.

When a Bedouin girl appears, claiming she was once the black panther the nomads worship, she is dismissed until decades pass, a generation of nomads die, and the girl remains a girl. In time, the next generation of nomads find their goddess in the young woman and begin immortalizing her as she digs from the rubble of their past ancient knowledge.

Once immortalized as the original sphinx, the goddess has been lost. She is asking to be found.

Can we dig from the rubble the remnants of our past and honor her, thereby honoring ourselves?

A mesmerizing goddess tale of ancient wisdom and understanding, this is as much our story as it is hers.

"Alicia Lewis is a true seeker who has found herself through a deep commitment to self love and self compassion."
      - Mindy Ray, owner, Healing Inspirations

"Alicia is a gifted, loving, and compassionate healer."
      - Dawn Omo, Reiki client

Also by

ALICIA CAHALANE LEWIS

The Intrepid Meditator: Connecting Soul to Self

Room Service Please

Restless

The Faeries Of Fable Island

Alicia Cahalane Lewis

ALICIA CAHALANE LEWIS is a ninth-generation Quaker from the Shenandoah Valley of Virginia. She holds an MFA in creative writing from Naropa University where her poetry appeared in *Not Enough Night.* She is the author of the book-length prose poem *nebulous beginnings and strings* featuring art by Shenandoah Valley artist Winslow McCagg (Tattered Press, 2017). Her chapbook, *The Fish Turned the Waters Over so the Birds Would Have a Sky,* a contemplative meditation on the origins of evolution, was published by The Lune Chapbook Series (Spring, 2017).

The Intrepid Meditator (2021), a self-help memoir, and the novellas, *Room Service Please* (2022), *Restless* (2023), and *The Faeries of Fable Island* (2024), were published by Tattered Script Publishing. A Reiki Master and meditation teacher, Alicia continues to live and work in the Shenandoah Valley.

aliciacahalanelewis.com

THE ARCHIVIST

The Archivist

Alicia Cahalane Lewis

Tattered Script Publishing
PO Box 1704
Middleburg, Virginia 20117
tatteredscript.com

ISBN 9781737521983
eISBN 9781737521990
Printed in the United States of America
10 9 8 7 6 5 4 3 2 1

Tattered Script Publishing: Crafting Cultural Creativity and Authenticity

Cover art and design by Emily Kallick

First Printing, 2024

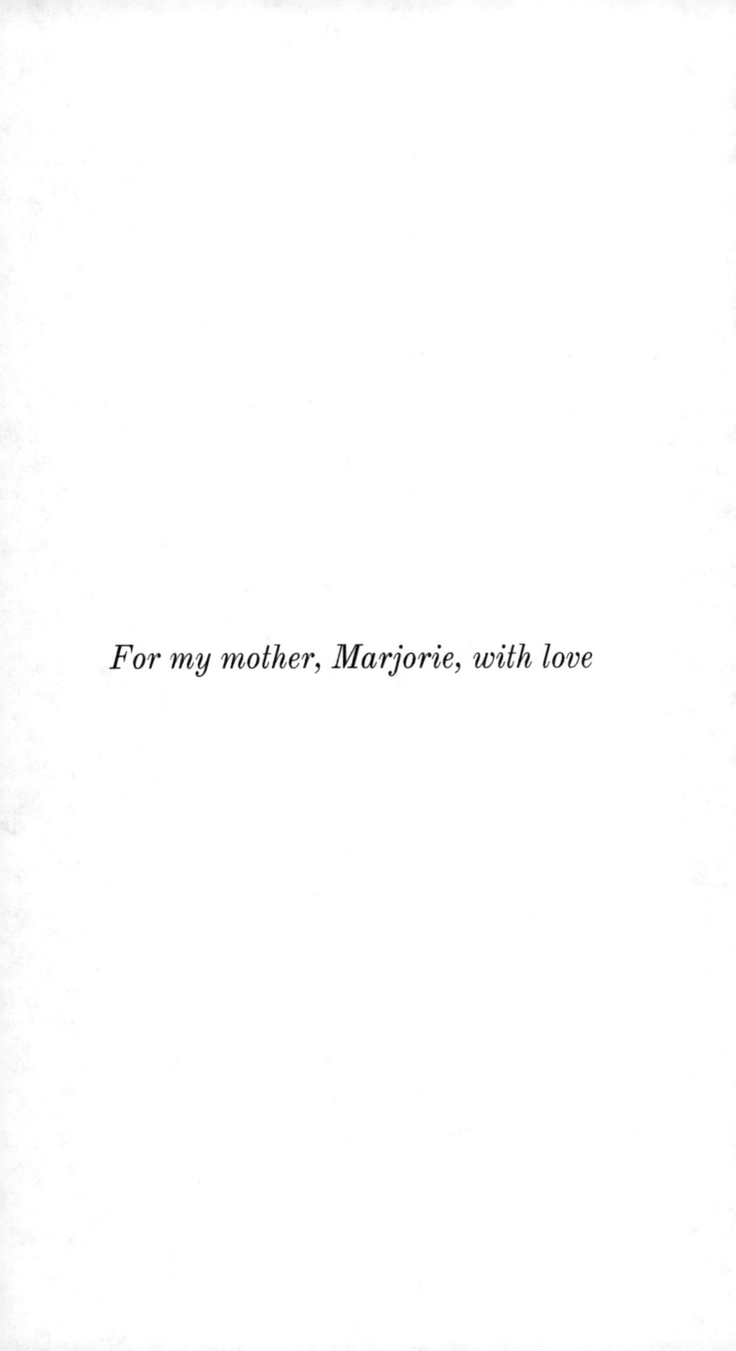

For my mother, Marjorie, with love

Prologue

I was born from chaos when celestial stars, bands of light, and sounds of intercourse screamed through the terrifying sky. Even though I did not wish to be born, I was born as a thought. I am a thought. I come as a young woman, a black lioness, a goddess, an empress, a queen, for you have asked this of me. I am a way-shower. You have made me so. I did not ask to come into your minds, or this desert, and make my way into your hearts—I simply arrived. And although this conjuring might appear impossible, this is how I came to be.

I arrived long before the bands of nomads who first pitched their tents along the river came. Long before the shifting sands swallowed our land and buried us whole. Longer still, before the monuments were erected and fell. I came because you needed help navigating these turbulent waves.

I will come again and again in language, creativity, and dance, for I am love. You will find me in the ancient artifacts, the symbols, and the dials, but I was not born to stay immortalized in rock. I am the way. I am your evolution—the modern equivalent of a ghost, a wandering soul, a vagabond.

Were I to date myself, I would rein myself in, and I do not wish to be constrained. I was created before time became a construct, and long before symbols and signs became a form of communication. I am a wanderer, I will continue to wander, and I will wander in and out of your hearts and minds with each passing generation. No monument of stone will do me justice, for no monument can solve the problems of those who have lost their way.

Be bold or be timid, the choice is yours. This land is tumultuous and barren without love. But buried beneath the shifting sands are the remnants of your love—each fragment a discernable piece of your buried past. Time is unimportant. My story shall be one for the past as it will be one for the future. The sands will shift and bury me, but I will always come again to ensure that those asking for help receive it.

One

Before time, there lived a mighty empress whose name was not important but whose stature was great. It was said that the empress, who traveled into the stories and legends of ancient Mesopotamia, Greece, and Egypt, was, in fact, a vagabond of sorts—a thought, if you can think of thoughts as wandering. We do not wish to bestow her with a name, for she is, to us, *the vagabond*. Never like the girls who are young and impatient, she has always been complete. She does not need a name.

This young girl traveled not in caravans drawn by shrunken horses, nor upon the backs of angry camels. Instead, she came from across time, as if the wind had carried her from a golden palace far away and out of reach from the praying souls who looked to her for help. Without a name, the girl thought she could never be corralled, but like the wind that could be caught in a large billowing sail, she, too, became caught when the notion of her materialized. Once a friend to all, the goddess is now lost. She is memorialized in paintings and sculptures, but that is not who she is. She cannot be contained. Her words are not words, but symbols. Her breath is not from her lungs and her back cannot carry. She is a way, a knowing, and her vision—the truth.

She stands amid the toppled stones, but it is not her place to explain what cannot be explained. It is not her way to suppress or to implore but to live in harmony so that others may see themselves through her. Some have turned our vagabond into a goddess, a priestess, a conjurer of spells and fantasies, but this is because they cannot find themselves and must use her to explain life. Who gets created this way from lands so far away that they are unimaginable? Whose mind determines the look, the sound, and the veil that she must hide behind? Or did she uncover herself? Once. And is she looking to do so again? Can this be why there are ancient pilgrimage sites and stone temples devoted to her? Is it because she once asked us to know her just as she has asked us to know ourselves?

We are besotted with her. Perhaps if she had not been subjected to the fallacy of Earth, she would not understand destruction and loss. She might know heartbreak and frustration, having come from a golden palace far from here that broke apart when she was exposed, but that will be explained later. This is an ancient story. It is ours. And it might be hers.

Two

The winds shift, and when we first glimpse the vagabond she is standing alone. Her head is shorn and her feet are bare. She rakes her slender fingers over the folds of her dark tunic and speaks. "Halt! Who goes forward toward this ruin? Explain yourselves."

We turn our melancholy eyes to a slim figure standing amid the collapsed mess of our fallen limestone statue. There she is, our wanderer, lifting her hands to the blowing sand, the broken stone, the loss. We do not know this child for she has never before been seen in these parts. A seeker, we think, who comes to take a piece of the statue for whatever reason she thinks it will do her good. We don't mind the thieves who steal our stones because we are tired of building this temple, tired of watching it fall, tired of it all.

We have no reason to believe that a feline temple such as this will harm or help us. There is nothing left to believe. The wind is the wind. The temple cannot sustain itself. The temple is just a pile of rubble worthy of no one. We have nothing to say to the shrouded girl so we turn away uninterested, but the girl is curious and she speaks from behind her veil.

She directs a long claw-like finger toward us. "I said, who are you and what is your interest in her?"

She asks us to explain the purpose of the stones and we turn to look at the fallen sphinx. We shield our dark faces. We are not accustomed to speaking in chorus, but we are troubled. Our upturned hands have been made dark by the blistering sun, but hers are pure. She pulls in her fingers, curls them into her dusty robe, and stands taller. She looks as far as the eye will take her across this land of nothing, past the simple huts encircling the sphinx and out beyond our sandy, arid existence. She looks past our fragile farms and our battering rams, but there is nothing more to see. The fence rails have fallen.

"You live here," the girl asks, "in the middle of nothing?" She takes a step off the broken structure and turns her dark eyes to us. "You live without shade," she says as if to explain what we do not know. We are not interested in befriending traveling vagabonds. We dismiss her and tell her to go. We flick our troubled hands at her as if by flicking them she will understand that, like a biting flea, she is a pest.

"Go," we urge her, gesturing. "Go now."

The child is unmoved. "I don't understand this," she tries. "Who are you and where do you come from to be here amid this…" She pauses. "This mess?"

"This mess," we explain, "was once a temple to our feline goddess." This she understands, and she nods. Her face is white like the bulb of Earth—the root. She can no longer shield it from us. We see who she is and we see that she is not one of us, but we are not wary and neither is she.

The traveler straddles one of the broken paws. "Your feline goddess is a she?" she asks. We nod. Who are you, we think, that you do not know this?

She smiles as she looks down at our fallen queen. "Having come from nothing to become something," she muses, pointing to the river. "You can harness the nutrients and make a better go of it here," she continues, indicating the black silt. "Spread it like topsoil, annually, over the sand and build your farms outward," she explains. "You will have better results. More nutrients. More yield." This we know, and we smile, showing her our black teeth and our calloused hands. "Good," she says. She returns her attention to the fallen statue. "Why do you need this dead feline queen?"

"We don't," we explain, "but we are worshipping the night, the nothing, as you say, so that we will retain something." We nod and bow our heads in agreement, but we are tired of building her up to watch her fall.

"Who travels this way," she asks, "to teach you these things?"

"There are many," we explain, "who come to visit our feline queen and so we do this not just for us, but for you. For people like yourself."

She understands and nods uneasily. "I am just a girl."

"Your family," we ask, "are they traveling with you?"

She picks up another piece of jagged limestone and slips the rock into the folds of her dark robe. She looks into the whites of our eyes. "You are ignorant of most things," she says unkindly. "There are too many of us without our families and so we wander." She points to one of our men. "You. You should make sense of this for yourself and for all the others who come here without hope."

"Don't take any more," we say, criticizing her. "It is a lot of work to bring the rocks here."

"You bring them here?" she cries, as though seizing on the idea that we are fools. "What tribe is this? And you," says the vagabond, pointing to Grandfather, "what are you teaching these nomads? Have you forgotten?"

We look first to Grandfather and then to the girl. He is smiling, but she is not. Grandfather flicks his leathery hands at her to tell her it is time to go, but she is unmoved. "I am sorry," she offers. "That was ignorant of me to presume you don't know that you don't have to move rocks. Of course, you know this." Grandfather looks at her with red-rimmed eyes and frowns. "Others are coming," she says, lifting her slender hand and pointing toward the east. "Caravans." She doesn't understand what we already know.

The vagabond shakes her head in disbelief. "You want to build this temple up again? For them? Is that your intent?" Grandfather smiles a toothless grin, but the girl looks down at her filthy toes and asks, "Why?"

We are too tired to explain that this is what we do. "We build," says Grandfather, gesturing uneasily toward her pocket full of stones. "The feline goddess is our livelihood."

She turns this idea over in her mind and then turns to face the sun. "I have seen many who travel this road, but never before have I seen the hordes that are coming now." We nod gravely. "I know not why. For land that is rich like yours, I presume. More yield. They are an emaciated lot. Build her up again," she says with a satisfied expression. "Build her up again for them."

"You've come to tell us this?" asks Grandfather uneasily. "You've come before them? A wayward way-shower to tell us this news?" He is angry and spits. "We do not need way-showers. No need for thieves. Off," he stammers, touching his face where his jaw, broken from some long-ago tooth extraction, still pains him.

The girl bows unsteadily. "I know not what I am. I am but a girl."

Grandfather shouts, "Go!"

We step upon the ruined stones in our tattered linen garbs and take her arm as if to move her ourselves, but she bows humbly. "I will ask of you," she says quietly, "not to harm me. I am a way-shower, but I know not why."

Three

In time, if there is such a thing as time, the people come. The girl was true. And we all felt hurt in our hearts, for her and for ourselves. Our lands were overtaken by caravans of weakened tribes who had lost their livelihoods to the sun, to the insufficient rains, and to their enemies. By traveling west to us, and finding more soil, more rain, and our battered but rebuilt feline temple, we became an oasis offering them, by our own blind luck, something to cling to. We did not set our cap on this, but we became this, and this is more of our story.

The girl stays, and we are aware that the vagabond is unlike anyone we have ever known. She is not blind to what is, as we have been, rather acutely aware of what will be. Perhaps she will show us the way. We can easily spot her, dressed in her dusty black robe, among the hordes who grapple with their fraying tents in the raucous wind. She does not have a tent or a woven cloth to cover herself with, but she does not seem to mind. This makes us pause.

She is no longer unlike us by way of color, for the sun has altered her. Over time it has darkened her light skin so that for all practical purposes she appears less like herself and more like us, yet her strange knowledge sets her apart. She is alone among many who wander day after day to sit with the newly built feline structure. We ask the child if the stones she has been collecting will fit, but she turns the limestone over in her darkened hands and says no. "This sphinx is not the sphinx your ancestors built."

Does this vagabond think herself so special that she cannot share her recovered stones? She sits alongside the temple staring at the crude stone structure, the upturned face, and the crumbling paws. She turns and looks once again over the bustling oasis. We admit that, although there are more of us now, more mouths to feed, more land to till, we welcome these traveling bands of exotic nomads. They bring excitement and tales of strange lands far from here where men sing lustfully and women bathe in cool scented baths.

Four

Again, in time, if time can be measured, we are overrun by the nomads, their offspring, their bleating goats, and their mangy cattle. Our lands become insufficient and coarse. Grandfather dies. The wind returns in fierce gales. The sphinx struggles. She lists. The vagabond patches her up as best she can, but the wind is too much for our feline queen. In time, more time, the black mud cracks, and the temple crumbles to the ground.

After much infighting, our fallen feline is exhumed. To protect her, we transport the stones to higher ground, but when sentiments shift, our camp divides itself. The stones are ransacked and transported in bladder bags set upon our swaying donkeys' backs to be used on higher walls around our encampment. Some say we must block more of the wind. And the sphinx, our black panther, this goddess of creation, is gone.

Among the chipped stones we have used to build our city walls, there are ample reminders of the black feline. She appears from time to time when we least expect it. A momentary glance at a keystone high above our heads reveals her fractured face. We remember what Grandfather once told us—that the most important part of ourselves was in her. She was created to be celebrated and expressed.

We understood this because he showed us her face in his, in ours, and we recited the words he gave us: "Almighty goddess, maker of dust and clay, we beseech you, grant us salvation."

We once threw palm fronds at her paws as we watched her fall, but then we would rebuild the feline goddess again and again because she mattered. And we recited the words, "Almighty goddess, maker of dust and clay, we honor you." She was of us as we were of her. When she fell we fell. When she was rebuilt we were rebuilt—the rains would return and our wheat would flourish. Societies would either prosper or collapse into ruin by the rise or the fall of our treasured sphinx.

The wind turns sharp and gnaws on our nerves. We continue to debate the feline's existence and the reasons for her importance. We are troubled by the marauding bands of nomads who steal more of our stones to hold down their fraying tents. Soon our city walls topple, and the stones that once created the carved feline are further scattered.

Our vagabond does not seem to age. She picks up the forgotten stones with her long dark fingers and we know not where they go, but occasionally, when we are not too hungry or thirsty to follow her, we turn and lift our weary feet to go to her because she remembers the black feline. She remembers while we are failing. And so this is what we become—followers. We do not understand how we became this way. We were once prosperous in our own right with knowledge of the feline goddess, but as the temple walls have fallen so, too, have we.

"We built her up as you said to do and look what happened," we wail, but the girl is unmoved.

"You did what I said to do but that doesn't make it mine," she answers.

"What? How so?" we complain.

"You are old and I am still young," she explains, studying the numerous chinks in the city walls. There is so very little left of the stone enclosure that we don't even recognize it as a city anymore. It is more like a dusty outpost filled with competing merchants who haggle and price their wares too high for our tastes. "Why is that?" she asks. "I did not ask to stay this way and to not grow old alongside you."

"Where are you from," we ask again, "that makes you so..." and we search for the appropriate word. "So malleable?"

She laughs. "I am not like the black mud you dig up from the river. I am not silt. I am me. A girl."

"You come from someplace unknown, child. Tell us. Who is your mother? Your father? Who are your people?"

"I do not know," she says uneasily. "I awoke one day to this. To you. I awoke one day to stand amid a pile of broken stones. I just woke and…"

"You're lying!" we shout.

"No. It is true. I was asleep. I was not dreaming. I was…" She turns to look at us. "Must this be the dream?" she asks.

We hawk saliva and spit the foul taste of our rotting teeth onto the sand. Feral dogs, mangy and flea-bitten, lap up what we discard. We are not ashamed to say that this is how we feed them. It is our way. In the saliva, there are leftover bits of food. This, we know. There is quiet laughter among us. Through our gap-toothed grins, we remind the child that we are old. "We will take the memory of you with us," we realize. "Do you not know the power of this?"

"No," she says, looking soberly at our malnourished eyes, our yellowing brittle nails, and our distended bellies. "I will bury you, each of you, with one of her stones," she promises. "With your feline. That way you can carry her with you into the life after this."

We are puzzled by this. "We do not bury our dead, child. We do not let their flesh rot this way." And in chorus, we cry, "We cannot decay the way you see a feral cat or a bloating ram rot. We are not wild things."

"Then clean your teeth," she says, sharpening a handful of fibrous reeds and pushing them onto us. "Clean your stinking teeth and do not ever let me hear you say you cannot rot. You are rotting. All of you. The stink in this place…" We take her tools and study them. There is familiarity. We know these tools and we are grateful for the reminder. "Where once you failed," she explains, "you must not do so again. These," she promises, "will prevent an early death. Didn't Grandfather teach you this?"

We are embarrassed. "No. We only heard the tales of long ago from travelers such as yourself."

"Well, now you know," she says clumsily. "And lest you forget your rotting teeth will remind you." We nod appreciatively and poke the reeds against our bulbous gums. "Go gingerly," she advises. "Go with caution or you will see more deaths. Here, let me show you," she says, taking one of her long pointed reeds and slipping it into the spaces between her teeth. "Go cautiously or you will create open wounds in the gums, and that, along with your abscessed teeth, will kill you all. Pop! Pop! Pop!" she says, clapping her filthy hands together with each exclamation. "One by one." She is not amused and neither are we.

"Why should you teach us your ways?" we ask. Many of us quarrel and remind ourselves that this vagabond is but a girl, and yet there are many more of us too weary to compete with the young merchants for a fair price that we find ourselves without direction. Without purpose. We are finding that we must rely on our auspicious traveler, for we have gone too long without the sphinx as our guide.

"What I am saying," she explains, "is that you can prevent death by cleaning your teeth, but should you die, for it feels like an inevitability in this dream of mine that you will, then we will wrap the body in shrouds of cloth and bury you. I will dig the space myself for you to lie in, if I have to, and send you home with one of these." Again, she shows us one of the feline shards of stone. "I will put your goddess into the grave with you and she will escort you back to the black of night from whence you came."

We are astounded and alarmed. "Shrouds?"

She slips her hands into the folds of her robe and explains. "I don't know how I remember this, but this is how we do it where I come from. The cloth is pulled around the body like this," she says, demonstrating how to wrap a shroud, "once the cavity is cleaned and perfumed. Your former body is a vessel to your next life. It must be clean, blessed, and buried."

"We don't know what you are talking about!" We laugh. "We burn the body."

She shakes her head. "I am here to show you a new way."

"Here," we beg, holding out our hands to her. "Give us your stones. We will clean our teeth with them!" And we laugh until there are tears. What fun, we think, these vagabonds can be.

Five

A piece of the fractured sphinx peers out from above the doorway of our battered city. She is only a fraction of a lost face, a large feline-shaped slice of an eye. We don't look at her the way we once did, but it is interesting to note that she still looks down on us as she once did all those many many moons ago.

We realize those were different times when nomads came to us because of her. But now they come to us for our grain and our barley beer. We no longer bring the rain like we once did. The merchants bring the rain, for each winter when it is time to sell their wares they conjure the rain so that people will travel across deep pockets of sand to come to us. Some who travel here to buy grain or fibrous reeds stay, for our land assures these nomads that they will have a place to rest, a mud hut to build, a way of being, and a parcel of hope. Isn't this what we all desire? A bit of something?

The young girl keeps to herself. She doesn't share herself as she once did, and we no longer ask her to show us what lies within the folds of her dusty robe. We know she carries pieces of the sphinx, but we know not what she does with them, where she goes at night, or what she eats. She is an enigma, taking nothing but our stone. In time, we will discover the truth, but the girl will never reveal herself. We will make her who she is.

The face of the sphinx is crumbling. This will not do, we think, but there is nowhere to go where the winds abate. Our walls will soon crumble. It is only a matter of time. Some of us want the child to take the keystone and rebuild the feline statue again, so we demonstrate to her in ways that bring attention to our past. We raise our fists. "We want," we shout. "We need," we demand. "We are first and foremost a feline nation, and we know this. Before you came," we continue, gesturing across the sand, "we were the tribe of the black lioness." There are more shouts and taunts and demands made. "We are the Black Lioness Tribe. Ay, ay, ay," we shout, "and the way to her is through us."

Six

The black lioness did not come from these parts. It was said that long ago, well before the sphinx was built and then rebuilt again and again to honor her, the lioness once adorned, like a necklace of sleek black fur, the dark oiled chest of a neighboring king. Elevated upon the shoulders of this mighty man, the lioness rode across the sand as his queen. The king kept her draped about him for all to see, but she was a dueling girl who did not take her sharp eyes off the man. One slight movement he made that displeased the panther and she could rip off his head. The king knew this. He, in turn, could not take his eyes off her.

He thought he was doing her a great favor by making her his queen, keeping her by his side, and giving her the title he thought she deserved.

Yet it was she who held the king bound to her, and not the other way around. She was the fiercest wife this man would ever know, and although he loved her proudly, the king was worn down by what he perceived as her control over him, so one day he brought her to us.

When the elegant, dark, and bearded king, dressed in his long black robe, strode among our band as casually as if we were great kings ourselves, he looked upon us approvingly, and without a word flung the unsuspecting lioness off his shoulders with one mighty heft of his arm. She was thrown far and hit the ground with a crying yelp. And then she was quiet. Stunned or dead, we did not know. Immediately, the great king kicked his horse with his calloused feet and turned the Arabian around. Dust flew high as he rode off as fast and as far away from those shocked yellow eyes as he could.

We turned to one another, and for the first time in our humble existence, we prayed for a panther. It was not that we knew who she was or what she was doing, having just landed so violently in our midst. We had never seen anything like her and knew nothing of a life such as this. Her toes were adorned with gold rings, and around her broken neck hung long strands of lapis beads. As we prayed for her life, we saw that she barely breathed. Blood oozed from her eyes, her nose, and the corners of her mouth.

"Ay, ay, ay," we cried. "Wake up." But the lioness was dead. A pool of blood lay behind her head, and as more blood seeped from her mouth and onto the sand we saw how ruined she looked. It was as if the sky had opened up and dropped onto us—this ruin. The rain did not arrive and our crops failed. Shelves of grain disappeared. We were parched and desolate. Cursed as we were, we knew we should not have taken the queen's jewels as our own or burned her body right there on the spot where she lay, but we did so. Those jewels have long been used as coinage for barley beer and seeds, and we know not where they are, but had we any sense we would have used them more wisely.

We spoke in hushed tones when we proposed that a monument be made honoring the black lioness. We acted as though no harm should come to us as long as we spoke respectfully of her. In reverence, we continued to pray to her, and in time one of our band sketched her likeness in the sand and we prayed to the black lioness for prosperity. We were cursed by the panther, and so to reverse the curse we prayed for forgiveness and invited her to visit us again. We built a small shrine, and from there we crafted a small three-dimensional sphinx. She grew in proportion until we could not make her any taller. The stones toppled. We built her up again. In time, her stones were repurposed and used to build a gateway to our burgeoning windy oasis.

We look up at that listing keystone as though all the wind has gone out of our sails. Should we seek her now that we are struggling once more? We are struggling, not only with our identity but with our purpose. Our sphinx has fallen and so have we. Time is nothing, it is everything, and our hearts are broken.

The beautiful king who kicked his calloused feet into the sides of his lily-white horse never returned for his feline queen and we do not know what became of him or his tribe. It was so long ago now that the ancients have long since died. But we continue to debate. If the king subjected us to this curse should we hunt down the sons of the sons of his sons and rain terror on their lives? Or have they all died by their own hand or by the hands of others? Dueling ideas such as these continue. Should we go find the tribe or stay and continue to reimagine our crude city?

As you know, we stayed. We continue to stay. We did not pack up our meager belongings and tramp about into an unknown to go look for him or his wealthy tribe. We have rebuilt the sphinx and repeatedly shared the tales of her magical qualities, for we are certain she brings us hope. We took an idea and ran with that idea, offering traveling nomads a new way of thinking. We asked them to trust us, to believe that by traveling to us and delivering sheaves of wheat or bags of barley we might give them, for this price, a piece of her magic. And so this is how we came to be the Bedouins in search of a black lioness once again. She has never left our lonely hearts. She continues to look down on us asking us to put her right.

Seven

The girl listens to our story. We see the wheel turn in her mind like the wheel that turns a mighty land such as ours toward the sun and then away from it. If there is darkness there will again be light, and we pray every day that we will be brought once more to the light. We pray for the wheel to turn. She stumbles over the sand. "I have heard more fantastical tales than this," she says uneasily. "What simpletons you all are that you and your ancestors should worship a murdered panther."

We are not amused. "You have no idea what it is like to go from prosperity and ease to this," we say, gesturing toward the greedy merchants. "Soon there will be more of them than us. And our ideas, and our stories...poof," we hiss, tossing our gnarled hands into the air. "They will be lost."

"It is because you know of only one foolish way when there are so many other ways to think. Curse yourselves if you believe in black magic. Or not. I see neither a gain nor a loss." She turns to go, but then looks back at us and bends sharply to the ground. We watch intently as she struggles to draw herself up again. "Your story haunts me," she admits. "I wish I had not heard it."

We smile. "You cannot have it both ways, child." She nods. "Come back to us. Sit," we say, gesturing to our fraying reed mats. "Slither not this way and that. There is more to tell you about the great queen, the black lioness."

She shakes her head. "No. It is too much. I do not like stories."

"Child," we cry, "this is not a story. It is true."

"A story still," she says, taunting us with those beautiful doe-like eyes. "Who do you think I am?" We shrug. "I am she," she whispers. "The black lioness." We watch, disbelieving, as she falls to the ground where she holds her trembling hands to her head as though she bleeds. She cries, "I know it. I see it."

We are alarmed. What child tells us this? Our traveler who does not falter, who does not age, who goes alone across our sand night after night? No. She may be an enigma, but she is not our feline queen.

"Forgive me," she says, kissing the ground. "Forgive my impulses. I am unnerved."

"Are you mad?" we ask.

"No, not mad," she answers quietly. "But I saw the broken neck and the long strands of beads coiled tightly around her. I felt something just then akin to death. I felt the blood in my mouth and the..."

"Madness," we cry.

"Possibly," she says, picking herself up and turning away. "It is the heat. The wind. Possibly, it is all madness."

"Are you cursed?" we ask.

"I know not," she answers truthfully. "But I saw myself adorned in gold. I saw the many rings upon my toes, the sheaves of wheat upon my crown, and I tasted the grain I once held in my mouth—the offering to life everlasting. I have this," she says, pulling from her black robe a single bright blue bead. It sits squarely in the palm of her hand. "I found this amid the rubble of your forgotten sphinx. I do not know if it is something. I only thought…it might be."

"Dear child," we say uneasily. "You say you found…"

"I did. I was not looking for this but for more stones. Only I saw this and thought maybe…I don't know," she tries. "It looked pretty."

We are stunned. "It must be a lapis bead from the black queen's collar." She turns the blue bead over in her dusty hand. "Yes," we say, extending our weathered palms toward hers. "Lapis is rare. You have found something very rare indeed. It is not from these parts."

"I thought as much. No one here carries this kind of wealth."

"No," we conclude. "No one carries the weight of such a treasure on their shoulders. Not us."

"I suggest we dig below the fallen sphinx," she says, "and see what else we can find."

"Yes," we say, whispering among ourselves. "Why have we never thought of this?" She tucks the lapis bead back into the folds of her robe as we consider her anew. "What else do you have in there?"

She lifts her heels as if to go, but then stops. "You covet this, don't you?" she says, glancing around. "You covet what I now have."

We are guilty. "Our child, we are concerned for you. What else do you carry?"

"I carry only the pieces of myself," she says bowing. There is a moment of hesitation, but she says nothing more.

"Why have you kept this secret from us?" we ask concerned.

"I have not kept anything from you. I know nothing of what you may or may not covet. Your ways are not mine."

"But our queen," we say, haunted by this girl who holds a gift from the black panther, "is now asking us to bow?"

"To me? I know not," she answers truthfully. "I do not know what, if anything, I am asking."

"Strange girl. Very strange indeed. Take us to the ruin," we say, picking up our fraying mats. "We need more answers."

Eight

Land such as ours shifts. The sands blow first one way and then the next. Land that was once exposed is suddenly covered over in a matter of minutes, and land that was once covered can just as easily become exposed. We know this. It is no wonder our vagabond has found the lapis. The land bends for her. We think about this, how the land has opened itself to her, how she has found what we covet, and what this might mean to our aging clan. We are lost, our feline stories are lost, but here is a girl who comes to us out of the blue, metaphorically speaking, who wears a long dark robe much like a panther wears black fur, and is now in possession of one of her lost jewels. It is almost too much to fathom. Who is she?

She tucks her robe under her and stoops low to the ground as she begins to dig through the forgotten rubble. "I have heard tales that you can be buried alive if you dig too deep. The sand will fall upon you, and within a blink of an eye, it will bury you alive. We must be careful," she says, using those long steady fingers to claw at the ground. She is unnerving us and we step away from the pit. It is not something we had considered, but we see now that she has been busy here, for there are spaces where the sand has been moved and piled into the far corners of the site.

"You did this?" we ask, looking aghast at the amount of rubble she has singlehandedly moved aside.

She lifts her hand to her face to shield her eyes from the sun. "Did what?"

"This," we say, indicating the mess.

"I have little to do that interests me," she admits, "so I look."

"What kind of stones are you looking for?"

She glances into the pit. "Those that were left behind."

"There are many stones here," we realize. "So many more than we ever saw before."

"That is because I pushed aside a top layer of sand and *poof*," she says, smiling and showing us her sturdy teeth, "these ancient stones appeared."

We shake our heads in bewilderment but crouch low to the ground and get to work. We do not have the long steady fingers that the child has so our work is slow and inefficient. She moves more sand than the whole of us together. It is a hot and tedious job. Many of us complain. Many more of us sit and watch. Those who crouch low to the ground with their knees bent and their hands over their heads, who watch through narrowing eyes and do not help, cannot claim the treasure. This is the rule. When they tire of watching and begin to covet, they resume digging, but when they do their clumsy feet push the sand walls back down and we must begin again.

The girl does not become agitated like the rest of us. She simply begins again. We are spooked, but we keep our thoughts to ourselves. She is not one of us and we know it.

Nine

The days pass and many more of us object to the tedious work. We have more important things to do than sift through sand so we rescind our stake in the treasure. It is beneath us to work this way. We are not accustomed to digging. Still, many more days pass, and the child tosses debris up from the holes into gargantuan piles. "This is ancient rock," she says, "from a river." Many more of us give up on the idea of treasure buried in the dry riverbed and return to our huts. The sun is hot.

This is where she spends her days and nights. Should we need the girl we know where to look, but we have other things on our minds, like how to outwit the merchants who overcharge us for beer. We return to conjuring up more ways to outsmart them while she works alone to dig up the lost treasures of the temple sphinx. Our minds are on that lapis bead, but without a way to hawk it, we are too lazy to travel across the barren sand. Let her have it, we think. Let her have her fun.

Many moons pass. We are disinterested in the girl, and what she has up her sleeve, so we no longer follow her out to the ancient riverbed. That pile of rubble is just rubble. As we watch our territory be taken over by thieves and wandering clansmen, we would do well to remember our veneration of the sphinx who will shield us from harm. There are more and more of us gathering to stage a revolt in hopes that if we tear down the pocked walls of our city we can rebuild the sphinx and return once more to prosperity. We know this prosperity will not be in actual goods, not the gold and lapis that the feline once gave us, but in the understanding that we belong to something much more important. We are the keepers of the Temple of the Black Lioness. This is our identity.

Yes, we aim to see our feline temple built again, and so we stampede the city, tear down the walls, and stage the coup we have so long desired. We are Bedouin and we understand commerce, but we do not understand how we have succumbed to such merchant trickery. Where is our identity? Our past? We tear down more walls and pull out the ancient stones. We must honor the sphinx. The child might not understand our ways, she may object to this temple, but we owe it to the black feline to honor her and put her back where she belongs.

"Almighty child, who has come to us from beyond these parts," we cry, "who comes from a forgotten land to dislodge us from uncertainty and steer us again toward our treasured past, we need the fighting spirit. Fight with us!"

She turns her attention to the dry riverbed and digs her way down into the deepest recesses of the earth. "There are strange occurrences down here," she says. "Very strange indeed. You can fight if you must. I, on the other hand, must make the discoveries you are too lazy to bother yourselves with. Honestly," she says, clicking her tongue sharply, "can't you, for once, stop all your bickering? What good comes from it? You are neither happy with the sphinx nor content with-out her."

We stop in our tracks when we look down at her in her pit of stone, for she is adorned with a crown of such glory we can hardly believe our eyes. "Are you mad?" we ask. "What are you wearing?"

She laughs. "Mad as a python who wraps her-self over a mongoose and strangles him with force. Mad as a hungry feral dog who cannot get what she deserves. As mad as the feline herself," she says, spitting sand from the upturned corners of her mouth. "But I am not so mad that I feel that I must tear down walls when I can dig up what has not yet been found. You look and you look in all the wrong places," she says, chiding us. "You look in what you think is your past, but no, your past goes deeper than plain rubble."

"Your crown," we say, whispering among our-selves, "is pure gold." We are certain of this. "You are beautiful, child. Stunning. Are you wearing the black panther's crown?"

She bows. "I know not, but I found it amid this pile of river stone."

We are the ones who are mad, we realize, to have dismissed this ancient river bottom. We step away from her and turn to go. "We can overtake her," we say plotting. "And kill her."

She fishes around in the sleeves of her robe and pulls out a large piece of black tourmaline. It is the size and weight of a small carp. "You might need this," she offers, handing it to us. "I don't."

"You don't need this?" we ask.

"No. I have much more."

We are astounded to think that we have left this child alone to dig in our ancient riverbed. "Who told you to come here? What are you looking for?"

The large crown slips on her head, but she simply pushes it back into place and returns to her stones. "I know not," she answers, "but I have memories and they are resurfacing."

We turn to look toward the pile of rubble we created when we tore down the city walls and then back again to the pile of stones that the girl has created while turning over the dry river bottom. "You speak in tongues, child. What is resurfacing?"

"The feline," she states. "I know her."

"We don't understand. Our black lioness?"

"The one," she says, adjusting her crown of golden wheat and looking us over.

We are spooked. "Go on with…with what you do," we say, simply turning and walking away. "We don't know what else to say."

She stops to consider this. "Your goddess does not need a temple. Rather, the feline is asking to be a celestial marker—an idea." We laugh at her, but the child continues. "She asks of us. Of you. We must make the sphinx a way-shower for those who pass beyond this world."

"As an idea?" we question.

"Build a marker," she says simply, "if you must. The feline died but did not die. She was transformed."

Ten

Light from the setting sun catches the girl's dark robe and turns it to gold. This light bounces off her crown and onto us. Does this make us way-showers too? "Perhaps we need more information," we conclude, watching the girl crawl out from her dusty pit.

"It is rather self-explanatory," she offers. "The panther is a way-shower. Build her up again so that she will become the beacon you first envisioned her to be."

"A way-shower?" we try, hesitating once more. "How?"

She brushes dust from her robe. "Give her stature. Isn't that what you need?"

We can't help but look at her hands and feet. "You are covered in welts," we say, alarmed. "Sand fleas."

Annoyed, she pushes us away. "You have no idea what I will put up with to achieve this vision."

"A way-shower," we say uneasily.

"I can help you build your monument to the feline, but first you must promise me that if ever I leave your lands and go elsewhere, you will transform yourselves. The temple is just a pile of rock, brittle and temporary. You must build her to become the way. That is what she is asking."

"Where will you go?" we ask, alarmed at the thought of losing our girl.

"Oh, I am not going anywhere," she says, lifting her torn robe and skipping alongside us. "Where would I go? Besides, this is mine," she says, sweeping her hands over the arid land. "I want to see what other forgotten treasures I can find."

She is cat-like in the way she slips away into the night, but we are concerned for her. We are concerned because a child who carries handfuls of lapis and gold will never survive out here. And yet we do nothing to protect her. We watch her. We know by the way she walks she is hiding more treasure in her robe. And still, we do nothing. We watch, and we wonder, and we surmise that there is much more to discover buried under that riverbed of hers, but we have walls to tear down and stones to gather. There is nothing to do but rebuild the sphinx yet again. This is what our ancient mothers and fathers did, so this is what we will do. And so we begin.

Eleven

Repeatedly, the sand walls cave in and it astounds us how easily the girl picks up her feet to move to a different location as effortlessly as we swat flies. She moves across the sand alone and in step with some master plan, because in time, when our children are old enough to move stones and help us rebuild the sphinx, we discover that the motion she makes is not at all simple. The girl has begun to make distinct patterns on the ground. Whether it is the outline of an underground cave, a large rock formation, or a deep seabed, we know not, but our vagabond will tell us these things. She knows.

When our children ask to dig holes alongside her instead of piling rocks, we refuse them. We do not want our children to fall into the pits and be swallowed whole. No. They must never dig, we demand, as we put the stones into their hands and remind them that they must build. Our sphinx is taller than any stone temple we have ever made. She is almost complete. We cover her with wet mud, and when it hardens we draw the feline features onto her, but the heavy mud dries too quickly in the heat and crumbles, sending the fracturing goddess to the ground.

We have heard the ancient tales of the black panther's death, and we hit the windswept ground with our overworked fists and wail, "Ay! Ay! Ay!" The sphinx continues to die again and again. Our children witness her death just as their children will witness it, and as much as we try to build her up to live, her death prevails. The black lioness collapses and the rains become less and less certain.

"I am remembering something," says the girl, showing us several pieces of carved stone. "These are not just rocks, but fragments of an ancient script." She shows us a band of linear markings carved into the rock. "You can just make out the images here," she says. "And here." We shake our heads. "These are more sophisticated than they appear. Do you not see it as I do?" Again, we shake our heads from side to side. "This is a form of language from some time ago. It was here long before you came to these lands," she tries.

She studies the ancient pictographs and reminds us that we were not the first nomads to settle by the banks of the mighty river. "There are underground riverbeds, former tributaries," she says, walking us out to her pits and showing us the underground landscape. "Tributaries are branches of the river that bend along rock formations and spill into oceans."

"We know this," we say.

"Yes, but do you realize what you are sitting on?" she says easily. "This is an ancient seabed. And your river is one of many that once came to the bed. I count three or four tributaries. You are living on top of an ancient civilization that was here before you."

We laugh. "No one lived below us," we say.

She shakes her head. "I have found ancient writings and more gold artifacts. There are pieces of molded metal and rocks thick with veins of black ore running through them. There is gold. And silver. And metal…"

We interrupt, "You already said that."

"We are sitting on top of treasure."

"We are sitting on top of the sand."

"Yes, but can you not see that below us, where the sand has now covered things, there is a forgotten city?" We shake our heads no. "Pity."

"Child," we trill, "we imagine you a fantastical being. There is no doubt in our minds. Perhaps you conjured this gold? Are you…?"

"I told you who I am." We look at one another and smile faintly. "And I remember long ago when I first came to the Bedouins."

"You said they were an elegant dark and oiled clan…"

She is abrupt. "I never said who they were. I remember I was wrapped in the arms of a great man. He was their king."

"You?"

"I," she says, pulling herself up to stand. "Here," she continues, giving us a handful of lapis beads. "Wear these on a leather cord to let others know that you are a rich nation. There is so much more below you. And wear these," she says, handing us dented bands of gold. "Be the clan you deserve to be. Be the clan that offers knowledge."

We are astonished, but we take the gold. "You are our savior," we cry.

"No. I am a child," she answers easily, "come to show you the way."

Twelve

Before long, there are those of us who respect the girl's ancient knowledge and those of us who don't. Our wealth is conflated and war ensues, but the child insists that we can each have a piece of the forgotten treasure. She begs us not to fight with one another, but to listen and learn from her. Not of our world, we are certain, the girl begins to convey authority. She asks us to rebuild the sphinx and use most of her treasure to adorn the crude feline shape. For this, we take her at her word. We do not know all that our ancestors once knew. We only know that the black lioness once wore strings of lapis beads around her neck and gold rings upon her toes, for this is what we remember.

"Your queen once had eyes as red as rubies," she says, putting a pair of gemstones into the eye sockets of the stone sphinx. She climbs upon a growing pile of sand so that she, too, is as tall as the temple. We watch her scramble up and down the shifting pile of sand and gasp as the vagabond moves with the speed and dexterity of an agile cat.

"Don't fall," we shout. "Or be buried alive!"

"I don't understand why you have never managed to get this statue right," she says. "There are proportions to consider."

We shrug. "We're trying."

"I think the ancients before you were pioneers," she offers, "and we should study them. We should remember their ways. I fear we will falter without them."

"Remember what, child?"

"Who we were."

We laugh. "You are otherworldly."

She frowns. "I was once adorned and loved," she says, turning to look down at her calloused hands, "and I miss him. I miss my king."

We shake our heads and whisper among ourselves. "Her king," we say uneasily, "who killed her."

"I scared him," she offers. "I was perceived as more powerful…" Her voice trails off and she turns again to look at all that she has accomplished. "I should go."

We shriek. "Go where?"

She shrugs. "I don't know. I feel I have done all that I can do for you. I have lived for too long upon these shifting sands."

"Stay," we urge. "Please. Our lives depend upon it."

"Your lives depend upon…yourselves," she answers. She looks at us and clicks her tongue sharply.

We don't understand why, but she stays. In time, as more time passes, the jewel-encrusted sphinx crumbles to the ground. She is no match for the wind. We take the fallen treasures for ourselves and hawk them for bigger barrels of barley beer.

Thirteen

You will ask how the Bedouin girl does not age, and how we, though our lives are simple, die easily. We live an average of sixteen suns. If we are blessed, we may live for thirty suns, but this is only if we do not die from some unexpected fever. A few of us will chase the fevers away with our rattles and our chants and live longer. Our lives are worthy, but they are only lives to be lived. We do not know of any other way until one day our vagabond recounts the meaning of her stones.

The sun is high in the sky, the heat unbearable, and the sand fleas bite. This is what we have become accustomed to. We do not know who came before us, but we have an inkling from their inscribed metals that these ancients were sun worshippers, as are we. But we think they were more precise in their measurements, and as we begin to awaken to the lost knowledge, we develop theories.

The sun rests on certain landmarks throughout the day. This is a fact. Thus, we surmise the land moves. We are an encircling sand desert. We begin to realize that since our lands move as they do, we will have repetition. Every new sun comes to us the same way and at approximately the same time.

We measure these sun cycles to calculate time and use this knowledge to our advantage. We can now prepare for a harvest. We can prepare for the heat. We can prepare for the planting. We can determine the best and worst times of a sun cycle to grow wheat and barley and to shear our sheep. It's rather uncomplicated, but this is new to us and so we rejoice. We celebrate and enrich ourselves with this knowledge. We drink more beer, have more intercourse, and soon babe after new babe arrives. We build bigger communities.

But wait, there is more. The vagabond continues to remind us of something we cannot grapple with—the sphinx. In turn, we go with her to the ancient burial site where we find the metals, the hammers, and the dials, and listen to her speak about their sacred meaning. Although she cannot recall the exact function of these instruments, she tells us that they, too, were once important way-showers. We scratch our heads. It makes no sense.

Fourteen

The vagabond grows in stature. We respect her as one of us, although we are certain she is not from these lands. This is something our ancestors once shared with us, but until we could see for ourselves that this young beauty does not age, we never understood. She exists outside of time and we rejoice. Soon our prosperous lands are not like all the other parched lands around us. This is something we celebrate, and over the course of many more suns, we adhere to a new way of thinking. The way opens.

We find our footing as she continues to dig. The stones reveal more ancient knowledge, and our enthusiasm for our land grows. Each time she comes up from her pit she brings with her another piece of our past. These are the pieces of a life once lived, but as we understand it, these lands were underwater, or at the very least on the shore of a mighty tributary. It is as though the sands pushed out all the life, covered it over, and put this civilization to sleep.

As the girl digs more shards from the ancient river, she says she is beginning to realize her true self, and that she must be looking through the rubble for some lost piece. She sifts through bladder bags of sand in search of her king, some remnant of him, some relic, a memory, and we begin to understand her. She aches.

We don't understand the desire to dig this deep into the past, but that is because we are solely focused on getting elsewhere. And fast. We need more cow dung for fuel. We don't have time to dig. We need more water brought up from the river. We don't have time to dig. We need to bow to our god, the sun, who gives us our wheat. We don't have time to dig. In time, the child will enlarge her pit of sand, and when she does, the winds will whip up unsteadily, carve out more graves, and disinter our past.

She brings up the charred bones of others. Charred, we think uneasily. How is it that these bodies did not disintegrate if they were burned upon death? Why are there so many bones intact? We are unnerved and our vagabond shakes her head. This, she cannot answer.

"I have seen many deaths," she says, showing us more gold rings left on the thumbs and forefingers of the dead. "Here. Take these. I cannot imagine they are doing anyone any good down here."

"You want to rob the dead?" we ask.

"Your mothers and fathers, and their mothers and fathers wanted the gold. Don't you?"

"We do," we say easily, "but at what cost?"

"The cost of my effort," she says.

"True," we say, nodding.

"I do not think I am going to find what I am looking for," she admits. "I guess I have gone mad."

"Oh no, you are not mad. You are you. You are…well…you are ours."

"I do not know anymore who I am or who all these people were."

"They were our ancestors," we claim.

"Yes, but how far must I dig until I get to the bottom?"

We shake our heads. "That we cannot answer. Until you tire."

She nods. "True. Until I tire."

Fifteen

The blowing sands shift to reveal a series of small ledges. They are made up of soft rock formed by layers of deep sediment and are unlike the hard rock of the hills. The girl studies the rock formations and concludes that they were once part of a communal dwelling. "See the pocks in the walls," she says pointing. "I remember these caves. I remember…" Her voice trails off and her eyes go damp.

We turn from her, afraid. "You must not enter those," we say, warning her. "There will be poisonous snakes. Wayward spirits. Vermin."

She nods. "There is always vermin."

"Come back another day when you have the proper…"

"But I am here today."

We nod. "You are here today."

"We are here," she says, slowly raking her hand across a dusty ledge.

"But it is dark. If only we had a light," we conclude.

She nods and continues to run her fingers over a series of engravings at the cave's entrance. "This is another language," she concludes, showing us a series of encoded symbols. "It belonged to the cave dwellers who once lived here," she says, pointing into the void, "in another world beyond time."

"Look!" we say exclaiming. "There is more. Over here. And here." Sure enough, as we clean off the rock wall, we peel back more layers of our past. The sands have shifted just enough for us to find another series of engravings. "A difficult language," we conclude, studying it. "One we will never understand."

"I know this," she says uneasily. She turns away to hide her face. "But I feel as though I will die again. It hurts."

"Have you ever died?" we ask.

The girl closes her eyes to think. "Yes and no," she answers. She traces her fingers along the sophisticated engraving, a series of complex round marks and parallel lines, and unnerves us all by reading aloud the strange language.

"This is who I was," she says, studying the engravings. "Who I am."

We shudder. "Who are you?"

She runs her hands over the back of her neck and pinches her eyes closed again. "I am me," she responds, considering herself. "I was thrown to the ground where I broke my neck, and when I awoke I was dressed as I am. The king was gone. He left me to die." We shudder. "But I did not die. I died but did not die." She ponders this. "For I am here again with you."

We pinch our fingers to our noses as we have seen her do in an attempt to see more clearly, but we cannot see what she does. "Astounding. You are, truly, the black lioness?"

"I am."

"And you've come all this way?"

"It was not far," she says pointing. "A few days travel across the sand." She has a look of bewilderment on her face.

"But you've come from some time long ago."

She nods and returns her gaze to the engraved wall. "I came because you needed me."

"Yes," we realize, "we needed you."

"You needed purpose." We nod. "Direction. Understanding." She continues to read the symbols on the stone walls. "It says here that a mighty warrior tribe lived within this cave. Could that be so?"

We shake our heads in bewilderment. "We don't know," we say uneasily. "We don't remember this. Perhaps your king once lived here. He could not have gone far then if that was the case. You will find him yet."

She shakes her head. "No. It was not here," she says bewildered. "But it is a strange thing. I know this language." We do not question her. "I lived here before I became a queen." We ponder this. "I might die but I do not die."

We stare at her, uncertain. "Perhaps. If this is what your kind do."

"I do not know anymore," she realizes, "if I am a kind."

"You're the kind who cannot die," we say befuddled. "At least not in our world."

"True," she says, glancing over her shoulder at the carved dwelling. "I should go inside one of these dark caves. It will help me remember."

"Be careful!" we shout.

She turns and smiles at us. It is one of the very few smiles we have seen from her and we wonder if once, long ago, she smiled when she was with him.

Sixteen

Now that the wind has swept the sand away and revealed the caves to her, they consume the girl's attention. She is convinced that long ago, long before she became a Bedouin queen who wrapped herself upon the shoulders of her mighty king, she lived within these dwellings. The lost words come through her and she asks us to see her more clearly. She writes long columns of picture sounds into the sand as she translates the symbols from the cave walls. We watch in amazement as she draws these images. Her sharp reed moves easily and without hesitation as she asks us to follow along, but we are too lazy and would rather watch her do the work than do it ourselves.

Every once in a while a young student, encouraged by her teachings, will take up the reed and learn the pictures, but in time when he is with family and must choose between casting his nets or starving, he will choose the river. Always. The antiquities and knowledge of our past belong to the girl. She is the storyteller we rely on. And so it goes. Day after day our vagabond grows in stature—in importance. Hers is the reed we follow.

No one, least of all the Bedouin girl who once lived among these ancient cave dwellers, and became the feline queen adorned in gold, remembers the sand's ravenous power. Without warning the wind sweeps in one day and swallows her whole. She is erased. Triumphant gale-force winds push the waves of sand across the desert, burying our huts and eviscerating livestock. Swaths of men and women disappear. We witness this. The Bedouin queen has taken them with her to her underground grotto where they will perish if they are not fast on their feet. We are astonished. "We should have died," we shout, running back and forth across the sand. The whole of our township has been destroyed. "Why," we hear ourselves say as we dig for our children, "did we survive? Why didn't the queen choose us?"

We are devastated, yet we know that some things cannot be explained. So we dig. Days go by. We lose sleep. We cannot eat. We drink rancid water for we are too distraught to draw it from the river. We dig until our hands blister. "Child," we cry, "our Bedouin child!" Then as the moon of the first phase comes into view, and the wind subsides, there is acute silence. It is raw—this silence.

Without a doubt, the vagabond had become the heart and soul of our territory. We are destroyed. No one knew just how ferociously sand could rupture a life, but now that the girl is covered, our loved ones are covered, the ancient caves are covered, and the dials, the tools, and the gold are all covered, we are heartsick. We cannot just leave her down there to rot in the ground. The goddess must remain elevated in stature, adorned, and remembered. We continue to dig, but the sand is as deep as the river. She is lost. Our mothers and fathers are lost. The whole of our souls is lost. We try complaining, cajoling, begging, and grieving. Anguished, we run spikes through our feet. "Take us," we cry. We fall to our knees. "We want to go with you, our treasured one," we wail. But we were not chosen. We must remember this.

Seventeen

The child is memorialized as the feline queen of a Bedouin king who once killed her. We must help her live again. This is the story we tell ourselves. It is all we have. We know she does not live to die, yet she is dead. The very thought of this makes us sink to our knees and pray that she will return. In our grief, we rattle dry bones to wake the dead and wail, begging the child to claw her way out from the belly of the earth and festoon herself with new sheaves of wheat. "Goddess," we cry, "bring us your new life."

Within seven suns our prayers are answered. On the night of a rising moon, the moon of the first phase, a slim young panther emerges from over a rise of sand and crosses our path. It is not often that we see these girls come into our territory. We put our hands to our throats and watch her. She watches us. There are no words exchanged, but those of us who remember the girl, and remember the stories, touch our parched mouths. We repeat the ancient words she taught us. The black lioness turns to regard us. She is frightening, coming this close to our sun-bleached tents, but the fear is compounded by the knowledge that if we are incorrect and we let her go we will regret this for the rest of our lives. "Empress?" we whisper. She acknowledges us with a nod of the head. We all bend to one knee and talk among ourselves until it is decided. "We will follow you to the end of time."

The panther turns and looks over her shoulder. Her yellow eyes are ablaze. They beckon. We know she sees into our souls, for we are the ones who lived. "We are the new life," we hear ourselves say. There are no rings on her toes or bands of lapis beads adorning her sleek neck, but this does not dissuade us from packing up our meager belongings and setting out across the sand with her. Had she brought her rubies and her gold with her we might have stolen them from her. Who knows? Our bellies groan. There is never enough to eat. The wheat lies ravaged by locusts. There is never enough rain. We are in a state of chaos and so we go.

It is many days and nights of excruciating heat and little rest. The black lioness takes us farther downriver. When she stops to drink we stop to drink. She steps eagerly along the banks of the river, and when her steady paws sink into the mud, she pauses. She licks the mud from her toes, but we are unaccustomed to such cleanliness. We drink the water greedily. We do not stop to clean our feet when she does, but the empress does not seem to mind as she turns to look ahead. Historically, we do not question our Bedouin girl. We walk on.

Eighteen

In time, or in what we perceive as the notion of time, we pause when the lioness stops to consider some new fertile land. She looks out over the lush terrain and takes one confident step and then another. She sniffs the new air, and as we watch her we, too, sniff the air, but we do not know what it is that we are searching for. A sign? A way? The empress pauses. She circles our small tribe, one slowly maneuvering paw now crossing over the other, and pulls us into a tight formation. Something is unnerving about this. One strike and she will take out many. She is hungry. We are hungry. We are so tired of not knowing what it is we want to know.

"Take me," a young man whispers, bowing.

"No, take me," says another.

"I will go," says another emphatically. "The girl needs me."

The empress regards the young men. Their eyes meet. Time stops as she pauses once more. We have come a long way over many hard days without proper nourishment. There is desperation. Our young lads thrust their confident hands toward the black lioness, but she pulls away. She parades around us again, and each time she passes she steps in a little closer to tighten the circle. We beg of her. The young men make it a game. "If we are chosen," they promise, "we will..."

The men do not know what it is that they will do. In our desperation, we have failed to tell them. Mothers pull their sons away from the panther when the memory becomes clear. Suddenly, they do not want their sons to carry the burden of our burgeoning young tribe, but the men bravely throw out their sun-kissed chests to her, to cajole and tease her. The empress stops them in their tracks with one swift swipe of a paw. "Bitch!" they shout. She bares her teeth and they stumble. Some fall. She encircles our group once again until she stealthily closes in on one of our frightened youth. She lays before him, subdued, but the boy looks to us, pleading for help.

We shout, "Ay, ay, ay." She looks upon our filthy Bedouin tribe with all the authority of a radiant queen and smiles. "Pick her up!" we shout.

The boy is astonished. "No," he wails. "Are you mad?"

"Pick her up," we hiss, "before she devours us all." The panther steps in closer. She lays one clawed paw and then another down before the boy. She has singled him out. He is too thin to threaten her and the older men know this.

They kick sand in her face and shout, "Choose me." But the empress has found her heart. There is no more cajoling. She nudges the young boy with her black nose and looks up at him with those haunting eyes until we beg him to pick her up.

Panicking, he cries, "Why?"

We bow. "You are her king."

"No!"

"You will lead us all into prosperity and great wealth," we cheer, hoisting the panther onto the top of his shoulders. His knees buckle as he struggles to hold onto her, but we help him until she is better balanced. Easily, she nuzzles her face into the boy's straining neck and smiles. We fear he may drop her, but when the young lad looks to the mighty sun for help, his strength returns. He grabs ahold of her legs with his sunburned hands and stands taller. Delirious, we chant, "Rejoice, the empress!"

We are astonished. Never before have we seen anything like this. Certainly, we have heard the tales from long ago of a black lioness who came to our tribe, but these were stories. They had no bearing on us. If we think about it we can remember the stories of the vagabond and the thousand-year era when she did not die. But we are not accustomed to writing down our stories so we do not know.

The empress has returned, born from the chaos of a broken life to come to us, unscathed and in control. The boy is charmed by her, and as he pushes the panther further up onto his shoulders, we know he will steady himself and carry her without pause. She has chosen wisely. A boy can grow to love without fear. He will be with her until the end of time and prosperity will be ours for the taking.

Nineteen

We watch through a thin veil of hope as the young man asks of his queen. Is she comfortable? Would she like something to eat? Where would she like to lie down to rest? Under this shade tree or that one? As she answers him, we begin to understand just why we have followed her. She has brought us to more fertile ground. There is more shade. The boy instructs us to dig into the dark soil and plant wheat. We do as he says. He instructs us to build huts from the coarse river reeds and to shade ourselves with angled roofs. We do as he says for we know that the empress has whispered these things to him. He then instructs us to build a monument to her.

"Why must we immortalize her," we complain, "when she is here with us?"

He shrugs. "Because you will need her when she is gone."

"You barbarian," we shout, tearing the panther from his arms. "You piece of dung! She must not leave us! We are the chosen ones." The empress pulls away and bares her sharp teeth. "You cannot kill her, you fool! You will ruin us! What kind of ignorant ass are you? You must carry her."

The king is resolute. "She cannot live forever…"

"But she will," we explain. "On the tops of your shoulders."

"I am the king. I know…"

"No!" we hiss. "She is the queen and you will do her bidding, for we are the tribe of the black lioness."

"I am the king of the Black Lioness Tribe," he says angered, "and your queen and I will lead you all into prosperity and great wealth." The king lifts his palms to the sun and stands resolutely. "The god brings me his wisdom, a new life, a brand new crop of wheat…"

"Our goddess brings life," we shout. "She brings us wheat."

"The god will be your trinity," he says, pulling the frightened empress to him. "He is the sun, the ground you stand upon, and your breath."

"No!" we shout, picking up stones.

"She is your breath," he declares, indicating the queen. "Your shadow."

We cry. "She is our light! Our life!"

Without warning, some of us hurl stones at our king. His polished hands fly to his shoulders, to his face, to his crown, and he falls to the ground, terrified. "I am the love of her life," he cries. "Help me!"

"You think we don't know what she is doing to you. To us!"

In unison, we turn to the empress and shout, "Are you the vagabond or are you a fraud?!" She takes a step back and lifts herself onto her haunches as if about to pounce.

"The tease! The flirt!" We throw stones at the bitch who has set out to seduce us. "How dare you!" we shout, throwing more rocks at them both. The panther screams in terror, but we are undeterred. "If you were planning to kill her to get her off your back…"

"No!" the boy cries. "I had no intention…"

"You cannot do this to us again," we shout, turning to her. "Whore!"

"But we must love her…" he wails. "She is the night. From where all light is born…the shadow….and I am the sun…"

"Kill him!" we cry, terrified.

Twenty

The empress throws her weight onto her hind legs and pounces, but she is light compared to our fury. We fling her off our backs and shout, "Now who has the power over whom?" We hit the boy in the eye with shards of stone and bash in his skull. Blood and bits of his flesh cover the ground.

As our dogs lap up the remains of the king, we turn our fury on the black lioness. "We know your game and we don't like it. You must put things right," we demand. "Do you hear us? Make yourself ours." The empress tears into the crowd. She screams and claws her way over the bodies of the fallen, bloodying them and scratching out their eyes. Some of us join the fight while others pull our dogs off her. "Bitch!" we shout, "go home." There is more madness, more pain, and more death. Can we trust her? "Go home," we shout. But the panther, if she is our vagabond, has no home. She is a nomad who has come to us from beyond time.

We turn to throw more stones. Why should we know where the empress comes from? She brings only misery, for when she is gone we are without hope. "Go," we hiss, "just go. Leave us!" We fight among ourselves and tear at our broken hearts. "If we kill her she will just come back to us in some other form," we shout, gathering some sense. "We can't have her spooking us again." We throw bits of her king to her, hoping that in her hunger she will be appeased, but the black panther tears out more hearts until we are forced to pick up more stones and kill her too.

Twenty One

There is silence. It is acute. The never-ending winds tug at our backs, but we steady ourselves and look out over the scene. Our queen and her king lie together in a pool of blood. There is more blood than we have ever seen before but we are undeterred. We curse the queen repeatedly until one young girl after another steps forward, offering to take her place. We watch one another suspiciously until soon we are whispering among ourselves. "We have gone for so long without a queen," say some, "why would we need one now?" Our conflicting voices are animated. "A king, perhaps, but not a queen," say others. "Never," a young voice shouts. "Never abandon her!"

There is so much blood that we cannot turn away but must stare in amazement at what we have wrought. We are not ashamed of what we have done, nor do we fear what will become of us. Rather, we are in awe of the blood. It snakes like a river under our feet and collects in shallow crevices of sand. It drips from the foaming mouths of feral dogs.

Without warning the winds shift once more; we pull our tattered linen further down over our eyes and watch as sand covers the remains of our queen and king. They are buried on the very spot where they were stoned. Tempest winds whip themselves up into such a whirling frenzy that we are blinded. We call out to one another, but there is too much noise. A ferocious wave of sand pummels us until we, too, are buried under the weight of it all.

We are gone. All but one. She stands among the dead, the half-buried limbs, the broken necks, and looks out over her new land. Tugging on the sleeve of her dusty black robe, she pulls a golden crown of wheat from the folds of cloth. The girl places it on her head and surveys her bright new territory. She likes what she sees. It is cool along the river, and there are ample palms for shade. As we watch her from some dismembered place in the dark sky, the empress looks up at our departing souls and smiles. "I am home."

Twenty Two

Born from some great mother who came before us, the empress stirs the passions of a country defeated by death. She looks out over her fertile territory with the power and grace of a Bedouin cat, until once more our people travel across the sands to be by her side. Day after day we arrive in droves, flailing, and in distress. There is more talk of her, more ideas, and more thinking. We question our past. Like a mongoose, we fear the empress tricks us, but she does not seem to die. She lives again and again to push her crown further back on her shorn head and goes back to what she does best. Digging. She digs and digs until the stories emerge. She once died, twice died, thrice died—but did not die.

We understand that like the mother before her, and the mother before that, and the mother before that, the empress prevails. She ushers forth new life. There is this profound comfort in knowing she will be by our side to teach us all she knows. After all, she is an archivist. A goddess. A saint. The vocabulary words will alter accordingly, but that is because we will continue to rummage around until we can see her more clearly. Will we ever see her more clearly?

There is this recurring idea that if we could build the archivist up, sustain her, and give her the stature she deserves, she will go on teaching us—our goddess who does not die. We shake our heads at the thought. We nod. There are ample discussions as to where to begin. The stories are conflicting. Many are lost. But we are an emerging territory, we consider, and we have the black lioness to thank for that.

We grow ample grain for beer, clean our teeth, curry favor, and trade for gold. We return images of the black lioness to our temple walls, for it is time we give the feline empress her due. We welcome all stray lionesses into our homes to protect them, for we know they bring great wealth. They bring new life. They circle our encampment, protecting us from thieves, and in turn, we honor them and treat them as deities. Perhaps they are gods? Goddesses? These words will be interchanged and washed over. God? Goddess? We think they are the same, are they not? Many say no.

"What say you?" the empress asks. "Can you not see me in the eyes of every feline?"

We shake our heads, for there are none who know what the mighty empress knows. She says her felines are our felines, and in time, for you must know by now that time is nebulous, the felines who grace our courts and shine for the empress are one and the same. We have no way of distinguishing one from the other, for the empress cannot say which of her is true.

"There are too many pieces of me tied to your past. I am in every one of them," she says, pointing to the cats. "Let it be known that all who go before me and all who follow me across the desert will be known as the Tribe of the Black Lioness. Build her up!" she shouts. "Build her taller than any queen before you and let her become the way-shower you have always dreamed of. Let us make your sphinx mightier and wealthier than any before her."

We are astonished when the empress chooses a king and asks him to respect her feline past. He is young and agile and can throw a horse to the ground just as easily as he can a lioness, but he would never do this. He loves his empress girl. We know this. We see the look in his eyes, the understanding when he regards her, and as much as we don't have this ourselves, we recognize that their relationship is one of equality.

He builds his empress a mighty sphinx—taller than any she has ever seen. By carving the feline into an existing rock face so that she will not topple, we wonder if it is not the king himself who has curried favor with the gods. Has he out-smarted her? Has he outsmarted us all? Alarmed at the thought that our empress has met her match in him, we bow, humbled by his wits. He drapes his mighty sphinx in both lapis and gold, for she gives him the strength and power he desires just as he gives her prestige for all the territory to see.

Time will mark itself in ways we could never expect, but there will come a day when the empress is pushed from the shoulders of her mighty king. He will not kill her outright, merely demand that the ancient sky-knowledge be bestowed upon him. He will demand the throne and become a great lion himself. But we will remember the child, the empress, the first feline sphinx, and we will recall the day her image was destroyed.

The sun is hot. It shines down on the young king from some great sky throne we, ourselves, cannot see. He tells us that he does not have to dig into the belly of the earth to receive his wisdom. He says something like this, the golden way-shower. Because the sun shines down on him, and him alone, this makes him the keeper of ancient knowledge. And so we listen.

We cannot recall his exact words, but he speaks with authority and tells us that because he receives the god's light (and he holds out his hands to catch the light that makes new life), then it makes sense to him that the sphinx, too, should be made in the king's likeness and receive the golden light. Images of a king ensconced in gold rush by us in a haze of impracticality. How did our Bedouin girl just get erased?

It is a pity, but those days, like so many, do not change us. We do not fight for her. Why should we? We count our monies and cash our checks. It is our turn to curry favor with the god when we bow to him, for he is mightier than a simple cat. This is what we are taught and this is what we will teach our children, who will teach their children, who will teach theirs, and so on and on.

Time has a way of forgetting itself, and the black feline will become lost until she is, on some windswept day, rediscovered amid the rubble of our past.

<>

Epilogue

The empress has been defeated. Was that right? We debate her existence and decide among ourselves that the king is the king. He deserves to have his likeness on the sphinx. We should write, the Sphinx, since he is a god-like structure of mighty importance. And the girl is, well, isn't she like a mother figure swaddling her tribe in the bosom of her soul? Yes, that is fine. Very fine indeed.

This is a narrative we can all agree upon. The empress, our goddess, brings us life. We need this. Let our kings choose their queens. Let us give the goddess a child, like herself, who cannot die. Let us resurrect her to live in perpetuity amid tales such as these. We will give her the life she deserves in monuments of stone. She is the goddess, the archivist, the way-shower. Our girl.

We construct the stories that we want to hear and that define the role of women, for this is what we, the levelheaded ones who sift through blowing sand, determine is best. We are not so lost that we do not remember the story, and we are not so agitated as our brethren that we kill her outright. We need a mother figure to care for us so we make the goddess our Mother. We put her back on the pedestal where she belongs and shower her with sheaves of wheat. We attach symbols of love, beauty, and life everlasting. There is a genuine desire for her to prove herself once and for all.

It is not surprising that worshipping a Bedouin girl would become fraught with contradictions, and so we are forever manipulating the girl into a theology that suits us best. With or without her, we are conflicted lost souls toppling our nations, time and time again, but the goddess does not shift. We shift her story. And the Mother Goddess is a good story. We are not so lost that we don't understand her, or the virgin for that matter. One ideology is as good as the other. Women are interchangeable, or so our stories go.

Most women do not appear to mind us, or if they do, they do not speak up. In this way, they create us as much as we create them. But it is the women who are not so cautious who start debates. Should they not want what we have given them, then so be it. It is up to them to teach us. Can they not claw their way out of the rubble and re-emerge to become the women they are asking to become?

My stories come from the stars. I might get a glimpse of a story idea during meditation, and from there, the words spill out onto the page as a way to share the meditation. *The Archivist* is no different. Is this the muse communicating? Some would say yes. But the muse is within. I feel quite certain that the muse is a part of our consciousness. If I believe that the stars hold ancient knowledge, and it is ours to catch, then are we not catching a part of ourselves in a star?

This story came about after years of reading ancient Egyptian myths, prayers, hymns, and religious thinking. I am not an Egyptologist nor expertly versed in ancient philosophy and religion by any means, but the takeaway from any ancient religion, if you begin putting the puzzle together, is this: Humans have been worshippers of the sun, the stars, the moon, and the direction of Earth's motion since the beginning of recorded history. Of course, I believe there is so much more to be discovered below the ground that will tell us about these early inhabitants of Earth, their religious beliefs, and their knowledge of other planets and universes.

We have found calculators (think Stonehenge), sundials, and calendars representing Earth's motion alongside images of the ancients worshipping the "heavens." Each culture has worshipped death as a ritualistic part of life, and these ancient beliefs were considered sacred. Both life and death were symbolic rites of passage. For better or for ill, we have developed theories about the gods from our ancient texts and illustrations, but our vision regarding death has been marred in fear. I feel we can take a page from the ancients who respected death as a passage. Nothing more.

We're no different today than humans all those years ago, except I fear we're no longer curious about understanding Earth, all she represents and offers us. Are we part of a larger encompassing soul journey, and if so, should we make more of an effort to abide by Earth's "rules"—that life is sacred just as death is sacred? I don't know. I'll let you answer that one. But I am grateful for the knowledge and understanding I have received in meditation. I am on a soul journey, and Earth is a waystation of spiritual awareness and ancient knowledge.

I'm grateful for curiosity. I want to dig through the rubble of our past and explore. This is why I write. I'm thankful for the words. They provide comfort. And I'm grateful for this opportunity to share them.

Acknowledgments

A sincere thank you to those who read, share, and enjoy discussing my books. Without you, I am half an author.

Thank you to my daughters, Sarah and Lydia, for your love and support. You've walked with me on this author's journey for a long time now, and I am grateful for your ongoing enthusiasm.

Thank you, Mom and Dad, for your love and support.

To Sandi Carslick, Sheila St. Hilaire, and Sarah Wergin, thank you for your unwavering support and love. There is much of this story that I am dedicating to you as well. My humble thanks for helping me traverse the soul seeker's landscape.

To Martha Bowden, Courtney Brinkerhoff-Rau, Kara Davis, Lisa Seaton, and Kate Wyckoff, my dearest friends, we've grown up together to share the happiest of life's moments, the disappointments, and the grief. It would be a lonely world without you. Thank you for cheerleading me on. I hope you can find your beauty and light represented in this book.

Cheer captain Amy England, thank you for waving your pom-poms so enthusiastically for me. You're such a huge part of this book as well. Let's keep digging through the rubble of our past to find the treasure. Thank you!

To my assistant, Emily Kallick, I am forever grateful. Without you, I would be lost. Your dedication and vision are so important to me personally, and to the Tattered Script Publishing mission. Thank you for being a part of this amazing creative journey. Your innate curiosity and encouragement are infectious. Your creative talents are unparalleled.

To my editor, Lee Bumsted, once again, you make my words shine! It takes a team, and I so enjoy the co-creative process, which you understand and respect. Thank you for your precision. Beautiful books are always possible!

www.ingramcontent.com/pod-product-compliance
Lightning Source LLC
Chambersburg PA
CBHW061221210726
48294CB00006B/1926